I HERO

D0298977

TYRANNO QUEST
ICE STRIKE

Steve Barlow and Steve Skidmore
Illustrated by Jack Lawrence

First published in 2012
by Franklin Watts

Text © Steve Barlow and Steve Skidmore 2012
Illustrations by Jack Lawrence © Franklin Watts 2012
Cover design by Jonathan Hair
The "2Steves" illustrations by Paul Davidson
used by kind permission of Orchard Books

Franklin Watts
338 Euston Road
London NW1 3BH

Franklin Watts Australia
Level 17/207 Kent Street
Sydney, NSW 2000

A CIP catalogue record for this book
is available from the British Library.

ISBN: 978 1 4451 0877 3

3 5 7 9 10 8 6 4 2

Printed in Great Britain

Franklin Watts is a division of Hachette Children's Books,
an Hachette UK company.
www.hachette.co.uk

How to be a hero

This book is not like others you may have read. You are the hero of this adventure. It is up to you to make decisions that will affect how the adventure unfolds.

Each section of this book is numbered. At the end of most sections, you will have to make a choice. The choice you make will take you to a different section of the book.

Some of your choices will help you to complete the adventure successfully. But choose carefully, some of your decisions could be fatal!

If you fail, then start the adventure again and learn from your mistake.

If you choose correctly you will succeed in your mission.

Don't be a zero, be a hero!

The story so far...

You are a member of a Special Forces military unit. You have been involved in many dangerous missions and have won many medals for your bravery. You are skilled in all forms of combat and weaponry. You have been recruited by Earth Defence to undertake a highly dangerous mission.

Earth Defence is an ultra-secret unit whose job is to defend Earth from attacks by hostile alien forces. The Earth Defence HQ, called Area 61, is based inside a mountain.

You have been given an amazing piece of technology to help you with your quest. It is a Defence Armed-Response Teleportation suit (DART for short). Not only does the suit have an incredible weapons system, but it also allows you to travel to distant planets and different dimensions.

Its inventor is an alien member of Earth Defence, called QTee. He is the technical genius behind all of their weapons and equipment.

↑ **eGun** – main arm-mounted, medium-power weapon, fires energy bolts

↑ **Needle laser** – arm-mounted, light weapon, rapid fire

↑ **Missile launcher** – shoulder-mounted, fires explosive missiles and also QTee's bombs

NAV system – a guidance system to help you find your way

Power unit – storage cell for crystals that you find

DART suit features

↑ **Speed function** – run twice as fast over a short distance. Also has "super speed" for x4 speed burst.

↑ **Net launcher** – arm-mounted, fires steel web net to catch and snare

Other special features:

Poly-absorption armour

Teleportation unit

Stealth mode – you can sneak past enemies

EARTH DEFENCE
BRIEFING DOCUMENT

IDENTIFICATION OF ENEMY

NAME: TYRANNO — also known as: The Starlord and Emperor Of A Thousand Worlds

HOMEWORLD: The Deathworld

LOCATION: Unknown

AMBITION: To rule all known planets throughout every dimension of time and space

BACKGROUND INFORMATION

Tyranno has placed his followers to rule planets throughout the galaxies and dimensions.

These governors have each been given a Staff of Power that they use to enforce their rule.

Tyranno has ordered that Earth is to be invaded and conquered.

Earth has already been attacked by Hurrikano, the ruler of Airworld, and Vulkana, the ruler of Fireworld. Hurrikano used his power over air to attack and Vulkana used her power over the element of fire to activate the Earth's volcanoes.

You stopped their attacks by travelling to both Airworld and Fireworld to defeat the two rulers. You have also captured the crystals from each Staff of Power. QTee has placed them in the DART suit, which means that you now have control over the elements of air and fire.

And you will need them, because you know that Tyranno will continue with his plans to invade Earth. There are dangerous days ahead...

Go to 1.

1

You are taking a test flight in the DART suit over the forests that surround Area 61. You are testing the suit's new fire controls by sending streams of flame shooting across the sky.

Suddenly from out of nowhere, a huge snow cloud forms around you. The temperature plunges as a raging snowstorm erupts. Icy winds blow you around like a rag doll. Ice begins to form on the DART suit.

"DART systems failing," warns the suit's computer.

If you wish to try to melt the ice with fire, go to 28.

If you want to use super speed to try to melt the ice, go to 45.

2

You swoop down and open fire on the frost bears with your eGun. You score one or two hits, but the others just keep shooting at you.

The frost bears track you across the sky with their guns. Two ice beams cross over in front of you, and you only just manage to fly under them. You know that you can't continue to dodge the bears' attack and shoot at them with your eGun.

If you want to attack using fire, go to 26.

If you wish to try to get away using super speed, go to 30.

3

Before you can give your order to the DART suit, your enemy lunges forward and bites you with its piercing icicle teeth.

The suit is punctured! You feel the ice cold grip at your body.

"Systems failing..."

"Teleport," you order, but it is too late, the DART suit doesn't respond.

Once again the ice snake bites at you with its diamond-hard teeth, ripping holes in the armour.

Then it takes you in its mouth, shakes you around and flings you against the mountainous sheets of ice. Your body is broken and you drop through the air onto the frozen ground.

Go to 49.

The teleport to Iceworld takes seconds.

The bright white light fades away and you find yourself standing in the middle of a huge frozen lake.

"Outside temperature minus 90 degrees Celsius," the computer warns. You know that if your suit is damaged you will freeze to death very quickly.

As you stand wondering whether to head north or south, you see movement ahead of you. Several white shapes are heading your way across the ice. They are travelling at high speed.

"Scan ahead," you order.

"FROST BEARS," replies the computer. "Highly dangerous."

If you wish to fight the frost bears, go to 43.

If you wish to fly away and avoid them, go to 19.

5

To cause a diversion you aim the gamma-ray laser at Arktos's ice palace and fire. The laser beam hits the palace.

Nothing happens. You curse QTee and his experimental weapon. Then suddenly all hell breaks loose. The palace glows bright blue and explodes as it vaporises and sends a shockwave across the glacier. Arktos's forces panic. They rush around in a state of confusion, firing their weapons and trying to get away from the melting glacier.

"Scan and locate Arktos," you order the computer.

"Enemy ahead, two hundred metres and closing."

You look up. Arktos is mounted on a battle mammoth and is charging towards you. He is using his Staff of Power to summon a huge ice storm. A raging plume of cloud towers up into the air.

If you wish to fly to attack Arktos, go to 7.
If you wish to attack him with your weapons, go to 22.

6

You head upwards and into the clouds. The wind picks up and hammers against you. It reminds you of the ice clouds you had to deal with back on Earth. You continue upwards, but the mountain seems to be never ending. Just when you think you glimpse a peak, another wall of ice appears — it is as if it is growing.

If you wish to blast your way through the mountain of ice, go to 34.

If you wish to try and find another way through, go to 37.

If you wish to head to Arktos's southern palace, go to 41.

7

You try to fly up and out of the storm cloud, but the DART suit fails to respond. Ice now covers your visor and is forming inside the suit. You feel yourself dropping from the sky.

Your mind goes numb as your body freezes. You smash into the ground. The suit explodes and you shatter into millions of ice crystals.

You are dead. Start again at 1.

8

"Super speed," you order the suit.

You fly at head height, skimming along the glacier towards the main entrance.

Suddenly, a solid wall of ice shoots up from out of the glacier! You have no time to react and you smash into it. Your head smashes against the helmet's visor. You pass out and crash to the ground.

When you gain consciousness, you look up and see a huge glacier giant standing over you, holding an ice trident at your throat.

To try to fly away, go to 27.
To teleport back to Earth, go to 14.
To fight the glacier giant, go to 48.

9

You continue to fire at your enemy but there are too many of them. They slam into your body.

"Evasive action!" you order, but you are too late.

Before the DART suit can respond, you are overwhelmed by the frost bears. Their great teeth rip through the tough suit and into your flesh and bone.

You scream in pain as the great beasts tear you to pieces.

You have failed, Arktos will invade Earth! To try to stop him, go back to 1.

10

The frost bear is in pain. It growls at you.

The DART suit translates.

"You have won, kill me now and let me join my brothers," it says.

"I will take away your suffering if you tell me where Arktos is," you reply. "In the north or the south? And do not lie to me."

The frost bear laughs. "It doesn't matter if you know where my master is. He will defeat you. He is all-powerful. He is in his palace in the north, waiting for you. Now keep your word."

If you wish to keep your promise, go to 23.
If you don't want to, go to 46.

11

You decide to head down the pass. "Missiles
ready. Automatic firing," you order the suit.
"Super speed."

The suit reacts immediately. As you hurtle
down the pass, the columns transform into
living ice snakes. They spit thousands of deadly
icicle missiles at you. You spin and weave, and
they explode around you.

The suit replies, sending streams of missiles
at the snakes. You hit several of the creatures
and they explode, lighting up the dark sky.

You continue to fly though the pass, destroying your enemies, one by one.

You come to a sudden stop. Ahead of you is the way out, but it is blocked by two goliath ice snakes.

If you wish to try to fly straight between them, go to 44.

If you wish to fight them, go to 29.

12

QTee presses a button and a large metal storage unit emerges from the floor. It is filled with many types of weapon.

He picks out a large gun. "A gamma-ray laser gun," he says. "Its light beam hits any target and sends radioactive shockwaves through it. This then causes the target to vaporise. It is especially good against anything with high water content."

"Like ice," you say.

QTee nods. "Exactly. But it's an experimental weapon — it's not fully tested. If you do use it — and it works — you must be further than fifty metres away from your target. Otherwise you'll receive a fatal dose of radiation. It can only be used once and it is a high-risk weapon. That's why I haven't shown it to you before now. It is up to you whether you wish to take it."

If you wish to take the gamma-ray laser gun, go to 31.

If you don't want to, go to 25.

You know that with your suit broken open, you have little time. Quickly, you remember what happened to the ice snakes. You send a stream of missiles at Arktos. He easily blasts them with ice bombs.

"You are no match for me! Give up now and save yourself." Arktos roars with laughter. But the thick smoke from the missiles drifts towards Arktos, blocking his view like a smokescreen. He cannot see you! However, you can see him with your DART suit's NAV system.

As he continues to launch ice bombs, you fly behind him and take aim.

"Fire!"

A stream of energy blasts hit Arktos. He drops his Staff of Power and, as the cold begins to seep through your body, you quickly fly towards it. You grab hold of it with your icy fingers.

"No!" he cries as he falls to the floor.

You snap the staff in half.

There is a great whirlwind of ice and snow as the storm disappears and the landscape transforms instantly. Ice and snow disappear

and the temperature of the planet shoots up. Grass and plants suddenly appear amongst the rocks and earth and all about you, the forces of Arktos are disappearing.

You stand over the body of Arktos. He is dying.

"You lose," you say.

He laughs. "No. I have completed my task for my Lord Tyranno. It was not about my forces invading Earth. I am merely a diversion..."

His eyes close for the last time.

"Teleport," you order.

Go to 50.

14

"Teleport," you order.

A white light envelops you and you find yourself back in the OPS room in Area 61. QTee and Agent Roberts and Agent Lee are amazed to see you.

"Why have you returned?" they ask.

"I took a bit of a battering, patch me up and I can return to Iceworld."

QTee shakes his head. "We can mend you, but there is no point now! You were our only hope to defeat Arktos. You won't have time to return and defeat him. The Earth will soon be frozen over and Arktos will become its ruler!"

What a disaster! Get back to 1 if you're feeling brave.

15

You send a stream of energy blasts at the nearest snake. It rears up in pain. Another burst from your eGun hits home and the snake shatters into a million shards.

The other snake hurls itself at you, spitting a volley of icicles.

You spin away from the deadly missiles and send a burst of energy blasts at the snake. They explode around the snake's body, but it keeps on attacking.

If you wish to change weapons, go to 3.

If you wish to continue to attack with the eGun, go to 20.

"Take me back to Area 61," you tell the NAV system.

Within seconds you are flying carefully through the snowstorm. The suit twists and turns, avoiding the trees and ridges of the mountain.

Soon you are back at HQ and in the OPS room. QTee and agents Roberts and Lee are present. They look worried.

"So where did that storm spring up from?" you ask. "Is the Earth under attack again?"

QTee nods. "Show data," he orders the computer.

The plasma screens on the walls light up, showing dozens of figures and pictures.

"The Earth's ice sheets are beginning to grow at a rapid rate. If it continues, the Earth will become a giant snowball! Plant life will die, oxygen won't be produced, seas will freeze up. All humankind will die out!"

"So who is responsible for the big freeze?" you ask.

QTee continues. "Intel points the finger at Arktos. He is the ruler of Iceworld, in the

Khule dimension."

"So it looks like I'm going to pay him a visit," you mutter.

Roberts nods. "Take your mittens, it's going to be cold!"

If you wish to head off to Arktos straightaway, go to 21.

If you wish to hear more about your mission, go to 40.

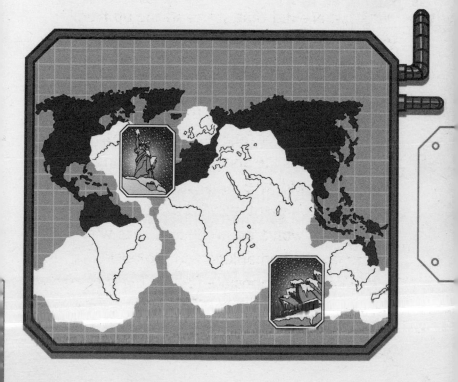

17

You aim your eGun and finish off the creature.

You check around, but no more of your enemies are alive.

Where to go now? you wonder. North or south?

If you wish to head towards Arktos's northern palace, go to 33.

If you wish to head to Arktos's southern palace, go to 41.

18

You know that you are hopelessly outnumbered. You will only have one chance to get near enough to Arktos to try to capture his Staff of Power. He is standing in front of the palace.

"Distance to target?" you ask the computer.

"Three-hundred-and-fifty metres."

You arm the gamma-ray laser and take a deep breath.

If you want to try to cause a diversion, go to 5.

If you wish to get as close to Arktos as you can and then attack, go to 42.

19

You fly up into the air above the oncoming creatures. As you gain height the air is suddenly filled with solid white beams.

"Frost bears are armed with ice-beam guns."

"Thanks for letting me know," you mutter at the suit.

The frost bears open fire again, and you are forced to dodge the freezing beams. The air crackles around you as the beams move closer...

If you wish to fight the frost bears with fire, go to 26.

If you wish to use your eGun, go to 2.

To try to escape using super speed, go to 30.

20

You continue your attack, spinning away from the icicles the snake shoots at you.

You target the snake's head. A burst of energy blasts hit the snake's head and it smashes apart. Its lifeless body crashes down the side of the mountain.

You stare into the pass and can make out more "columns". You order the DART suit to scan these.

The computer confirms your suspicions. "Ice snakes."

You curse. Time is running out. You wonder if you could try to blast a way through the side of the ice mountain and avoid the snakes.

If you wish to head further into the pass, go to 11.

If you wish to try to blast your way through the ice wall, go to 34.

21

"I need to get to Iceworld right now and make things hot for Arktos," you say.

"Slow down," replies Agent Lee. "Before you pack your thermal underwear, you need to know more about Arktos and his world. Without that knowledge, you'll die and Earth will be at his mercy."

QTee nods. "Arktos is more powerful than your previous opponents. You will have to think carefully about how you are to defeat him."

Go to 40.

22

You send a stream of fire towards Arktos. He counters your attack by sending a cloud of ice and snow from his Staff of Power. The flames are extinguished.

He is almost upon you as you leap upwards and over him, attacking with a burst from your eGun. You hit the battle mammoth and it crashes down dead. You float down onto the glacier as Arktos is thrown to the ground. The ice storm closes in and huge bowling-ball size hailstones begin to fall. You blast at them with your needle gun while Arktos quickly regains his feet. You turn to face him just as he throws his ice axe at you. It catches your DART suit, ripping open a hole in the armour. You feel a blast of icy air.

"Suit damaged..." warns the computer.

Arktos continues to attack, blasting you with ice bombs.

To try to escape, go to 38.
To try to repair your suit, go to 47.
If you wish to fight back, go to 13.

23

You nod and put the creature out of its suffering.

You have to decide whether the frost bear was telling the truth. Is Arktos really in his northern palace or the one in the south? You consider what it said and make your choice.

If you wish to head towards Arktos's northern palace, go to 33.

If you wish to head to Arktos's southern palace, go to 41.

24

The NAV system guides you to Arktos's palace.

Soon you see it ahead of you. It is a huge ice palace set in the middle of a glacier. Its crystal towers reach high into the sky.

The suit scans the area. "Main entrance guarded by glacier giants," it reports.

You realise that time is running out on your mission, how should you get into the palace?

To head to the main entrance, go to 8.

If you wish to try to find another way into the palace, go to 39.

25

You shake your head. "I don't think so! Show
me something that isn't going to kill me!"

"Very well." QTee puts the ray gun back and
points at some small plate-shaped devices.
"Chemical-thermo mines. Set them off and
they create an incredible heat. They will melt
most surfaces."

"That's more like it," you say.

"You will have the usual weapons and you can create streams of fire with the crystal from Vulkana's Staff of Power. And remember if you capture the crystal that powers Arktos's staff, you will also have control over the element of ice: that could be crucial in our battle against Tyranno."

"But you'll have to survive your trip to Iceworld first," says Agent Lee.

QTee continues. "I have set the co-ordinates for the snowy wasteland of Iceworld. You will need to make your way to the palace where Arktos is."

QTee arms the DART suit with your weapons.

"Let's go, before it gets too cold!" You step into the suit. "Teleport," you order. A bright light flashes as you are teleported through the dimensions of space to Iceworld and your battle with Arktos.

Go to 4.

26

You take aim and send streams of fire at the
frost bears. Their armour and fur bursts into
flames and they drop down, howling.

More of the creatures target you with their
ice-beam guns. You dive down and send ripples
of flame at the frost bears and they catch
light. In their panic to escape, the creatures
blast each other — putting out the flames, but
freezing them solid. You continue your attack
and soon your enemies are lying on the icy
ground below.

You fly down to check if any of them
are alive. "Locate survivors," you tell the
computer.

It replies. "One life form, fifty metres
ahead."

You head over to the creature. It lies
groaning, with its armour melting.

If you wish to kill the frost bear, go to 17.

**If you wish to try to communicate with it,
go to 10.**

27

You turn to fly away, but the giant raises his ice trident and thrusts down. The weapon pierces your suit.

Again the giant attacks, breaking through the armour once more. Time after time he pierces the suit's defences. You cry out as the deadly ice weapon tears through your flesh.

You have paid the ultimate price. If you wish to begin again, go to 1.

28

"Activate fire system," you order.

In an instant the suit heats up and the ice turns into harmless droplets of water.

"All systems restored," says the computer.

You are still being battered by the icy gale and visibility is minimal. You know that you have to get back to Area 61.

If you wish to use the DART's NAV system, go to 16.

If you trust your own skill, go to 35.

You begin your attack by sending streams of energy blasts at the two snakes.

They writhe and twist to try to avoid your deadly assault. They spit back huge ice missiles, which explode around you.

However, you take evasive action and reply with a volley of missiles. The cloud of smoke from the explosions covers the pass. Blinded by the smoke, the snakes crash into each other, plunging their teeth into each other's heads and locking themselves together.

You send a sheet of flame at the struggling creature's heads and they melt together. You fly by them and out of the pass, leaving the creatures locked in their death grip. The way to Arktos's palace is open!

Go to 24.

30

"Super speed," you order.

The suit responds, but the frost bears shoot ice beams that block your path. You crash into the ice and spin down into a snowdrift. Before you can get to your feet, you are trampled on. A frost bear's iron jaw rips through your DART suit's defensive armour.

"Systems failing!" warns the computer.

"Teleport back to Earth," you cry, but nothing happens.

Mercifully the freezing cold numbs your body as the frost bears feast on your flesh.

Begin your adventure again. Go to 1.

31

"I'll take it," you say.

"Very well." QTee mounts the laser gun onto the DART suit.

"You will have your usual weapons, and of course you can now create streams of fire with the crystal from Vulkana's Staff of Power. And remember, if you capture the crystal that powers Arktos's staff, you will also have control

over the element of ice: that could be crucial in our battle against Tyranno."

"But you'll have to survive your trip to Iceworld first," says Agent Lee.

QTee continues. "I have set the co-ordinates for the snowy wasteland of Iceworld. You will need to make your way to the palace where Arktos is."

"Let's go, before it gets too cold!" You step into the suit. "Teleport," you order. A bright light flashes as you are teleported through the dimensions of space to Iceworld and your battle with Arktos.

Go to 4.

You arm the chemical-thermo mines and begin your flight towards Arktos. However, you are quickly spotted. Ice demons take to the air and begin hurling ice bombs at you. They explode and send you spinning through the air.

You return fire and drop some of the mines. They detonate and begin to melt the glacier. Some of Arktos's forces fall through the melting ice.

You continue to drop the mines, but there are too many enemies to deal with.

You head towards Arktos, but are cut off by more of Arktos's army. You fight bravely, but it is hopeless. You are hit by a burst of ice missiles.

"Systems badly damaged," warns the DART suit. You crash to the frozen ground, where you lie, unable to respond.

A group of ice demons are quickly upon you and spray you with a liquid that instantly turns into a net of ice. You are trapped!

The demons take you to Arktos.

Go to 36.

33

"Set co-ordinates for Arktos's northern palace," you order the suit.

It responds and soon you are flying across the frozen landscape.

Soon it begins to get dark. You can just see the outline of a huge range of icy mountains ahead of you. They reach high into dark black snow clouds and you cannot see their peaks.

If you wish to try to fly over the mountains, go to 6.

If you wish to look for a mountain pass through the peaks, go to 37.

34

You blast at the mountain of ice with your eGun.

To your amazement, the energy blasts hit the wall and are reflected straight back at you! The DART suit takes a massive hit. The electrical systems burn out and all power is lost!

You begin to plunge through the air.

"Teleport!" you order, but nothing happens. Eventually you hit with a sickening crash.

Go to 49.

35

You switch the DART suit to manual control to fight your way through the storm.

However, the cloud of snow is so thick that you cannot see anything. You realise that you have made a big mistake! Before you can take evasive action, you smash full speed into the side of the mountain.

Go to 49.

36

Arktos stands above you holding his Staff of Power.

"You fool," he growls. "To think that you could stand up to the might of Arktos. You and your puny Earth are doomed."

You plead for your life.

He laughs. "Did you not know that I am cold hearted?"

He raises his Staff of Power and with a cry of victory plunges it into your heart.

You have failed! Earth is at the mercy of Arktos.

If you wish to begin again, go to 1.

37

You begin to search for a pass through the mountains. You eventually see an opening in the side of the mountain range. Two huge ice columns guard the way into the pass. You stare ahead and see more tall columns lining the steep walls of the pass.

As you walk between the columns, they suddenly move and the sound of ice cracking

fills the air. The columns are alive!

"ICE SNAKES!" warns the computer.

They begin to attack! They whip their tails round and you are sent spinning through the air. You smash into another snake's rock-hard icy body and crash to the ground. You leap up and dodge as they spit streams of razor-sharp icicles at you. Quickly, you reply with a blast of swirling fire that melts the deadly missiles before they hit you.

The ice snakes continue their attack.

To try to fly away, go to 44.
To fight the creatures, go to 15.

38

"Super speed," you order.

The DART suit fails to respond. You repeat your order, but nothing happens. Freezing cold ice is now forming inside the suit.

Arktos is upon you. Another salvo of ice bombs hits you. The explosion is the last thing you see.

You have failed. To start again, go to 1.

You spend some time flying around the palace trying to find a way in. Suddenly a great noise breaks out across the glacier. You quickly head towards the front of palace to see what is happening and give a cry of horror.

The gates of the palace are open and thousands of creatures of all shapes and sizes are marching out. Frost bears, ice demons, glacier giants and other creatures you could not have imagined in your worst nightmares.

Then the noise stops and Arktos emerges from the palace, riding a battle mammoth. He is holding his Staff of Power!

He holds it up and his voice booms out across the icy waste. "The attack begins!" His army roars in approval.

Arktos's forces are getting ready to invade Earth! You know that if you can capture Arktos's Staff of Power, his army will not be able to invade.

You have to react immediately!

If you have the gamma-ray laser, go to 18.
If you don't, go to 32.

40

"So what's the best way to turn up the heat on Arktos?" you ask.

QTee looks grim. "Arktos is very powerful. He is using his Staff of Power to break through the dimensions and create a world of ice here on Earth. Then he can unleash his forces of the cold: ice snakes, frost bears and snow demons are just some of the creatures you will have to defeat."

"Where will I find him?"

Agent Lee looks grim. "We're not sure. Our intel says that he has two ice palaces. One in the north of the planet, one in the south. We don't know which one he is based in."

"It doesn't sound as though it's going to be a fun day out!"

Agent Roberts nods. "You are going to have to take some very powerful weapons with you."

QTee smiles. "And I've invented something very special for you!"

Go to 12.

You set the NAV system with the co-ordinates to Arktos's southern palace.

You set off, but the journey takes many hours.

Finally, you arrive at the palace. It is completely deserted! You know you have made the wrong choice.

At that moment, you receive a message from QTee back on Earth.

"Arktos has begun his invasion of Earth — you have failed! There is no point coming back home because Earth will…"

The transmission is cut off. You know that Earth is doomed and you can do nothing about it.

You have failed. Begin your adventure again by going back to 1.

42

You fly towards Arktos to get as close as possible.

The enemy forces open fire at you. Ice demons launch grenades at you which explode, firing diamond-hard iceflakes. You dodge them and launch missiles and fire your eGun — taking some enemies out. Arktos is now only fifty metres away!

"Target lock. Fire!" you order the suit.

The deadly laser beam shoots out, hitting Arktos in the chest. There is a moment's pause, then the whole glacier erupts as everything around you is vaporised. Arktos is dead!

Your joy quickly turns to despair. Too late, you remember what QTee told you. The radiation blast from the gamma-ray gun hits you. The DART suit is ripped open and your body is atomised.

You have beaten Arktos, but lost your life. If you wish to begin again, go to 1.

"We didn't come here to make friends," you say. "Launch missiles!"

The deadly missiles streak away into the air. The frost bears speed up and charge straight towards you.

Some frost bears are hit by the missiles, but as the others get closer they open their great jaws. Huge razor-sharp teeth glisten in the light. They howl as they move in for the attack.

You aim your eGun and take out the first creature with a volley of well-aimed shots.

You take down another frost bear, but the others keep coming — as they charge you realise that you are badly outnumbered.

If you wish to try to escape, go to 19.

To stand your ground and continue the fight, go to 9.

44

Before you can get airbourne, one of the snakes wraps its body around you, pinning your arms against your body. You try to escape, but the creature's grip is too strong. You are trapped in the coils!

The creature smashes you against the wall of ice, practically knocking you out. You feel blood running down your face. The other snake moves in for the kill, with its mouth wide open and its fangs ready to strike.

If you wish to teleport back to Earth, go to 14.

If you wish to try to fight your way out of the situation, go to 3.

45

"Activate super speed," you order.

You fly faster through the freezing gale, but ice continues to cover the DART suit, weighing it down.

The computer's voice sounds weak. "S-y-s-t-e-m-s failing..."

You have to act immediately!

If you want to try to fly out of the cloud, go to 7.

If you decide to activate the suit's fire system, go to 28.

46

You shake your head. "I don't think I will waste any more energy on you."

You turn, but as you do, the creature leaps up at you and its great jaws bite into your suit, ripping open a gaping hole.

You shoot the creature and it drops dead, but you are in trouble! You feel your body beginning to freeze with the cold.

"Systems failing," warns the DART suit.

"Teleport to Earth," you order.

"Teleport malfunction..."

You try to fly away, but the suit doesn't respond.

The cold has destroyed the computer's systems and is eating at your body. You sink to the ground and curse at the fact that you didn't keep your word...

Go to 49.

47

To give you time to mend the suit you know that you have to get away from Arktos.

"Super speed," you order.

But before the suit can respond, you are hit by another ice bomb.

"Systems failing," warns the suit.

You are helpless. Arktos sends more ice bombs towards you. They explode, sending you to oblivion.

If you wish to begin again, go to 1.

48

Before the glacier giant can attack, you send a sheet of flame into his body.

He cries out in pain, and staggers away. You leap up and send a volley of energy blasts at your enemy. The giant has no defence against such an attack and he falls to the floor, dead.

You realise that more giants are in your way — you cannot head straight to the main entrance, you will have to find another way in.

Go to 39.

49

You lie helpless on the frozen ground. Your
suit is broken open and you feel the icy cold
creeping through your veins, chilling your
blood.

You try to get up, but it is hopeless. You
know that you are going to freeze to death.
You lie waiting for the end.

**You have paid the ultimate price. If you
wish to begin again, go to 1.**

50

There is a flash of light, a roaring sound and
then you are back in the OPS room in Area 61,
with QTee and the agents.

You hand over the power crystal from
Arktos's staff. This will now give you power
over the elements of snow and ice.

You give an account of your adventures to
QTee and agents Lee and Roberts.

"I wonder what Arktos meant about just
being a diversion?" says Agent Roberts.

You shrug. "I'm sure that we will find out
soon enough."

QTee nods grimly. "You're right. We still have to deal with Tyranno. The war is not yet won..."

You succeeded! You are a hero!
Thanks to you, Earth is safe...
...for the time being...

DECIDE YOUR OWN DESTINY

I HERO

TYRANNO QUEST
EARTH ATTACK
Steve Barlow - Steve Skidmore

EDGE

As Tyranno prepares to unleash his alien armies
on Earth, only one person stands in his way – YOU!
Your quest is to save the planet by defeating Tyranno.
But the evil Starlord is strong and powerful. It will
take all your skill and strength to free the universe
from the grip of Tyranno. All you need to
do is make the right choices...

You are the hero of this book.
Only you can decide your own destiny...

Discover some of the aliens from EARTH ATTACK...

Element monster — this giant hulk attacks Area 61 using its bare hands!

Skeleton droids — part of Tyranno's army on the Deathworld. They're armed and dangerous!

Robo snakes —
not the sort you'd
want as a pet. These
guys launch missiles
from their mouths.

Alien zombies —
they might look slow, but they pack a punch.
These are the best alien zombies, brought
together from across the universe.

About the 2Steves

"The 2Steves" are
Britain's most popular
writing double act
for young people,
specialising in comedy
and adventure. They
perform regularly in schools and libraries,
and at festivals, taking the power of words
and story to audiences of all ages.

Together they have written many books,
including the *Crime Team* and *iHorror* series.

About the illustrator: Jack Lawrence

Jack Lawrence is a successful freelance
comics illustrator, working on titles such as
A.T.O.M., Cartoon Network, *Doctor Who
Adventures*, *2000 AD*, *Gogos Mega Metropolis*
and *Spider-Man Tower of Power*. He also works
as a freelance toy designer.

Jack lives in Maidstone in Kent with
his partner and two cats.

Want to read more "You Are The Hero" adventures? Well, why not try these...

Also by the 2Steves: iHorror
Fight your fear. Choose your fate.

978 1 40830 985 8 pb
978 1 40831 476 0 eBook

978 1 40830 986 5 pb
978 1 40831 477 7 eBook

978 1 40830 988 9 pb
978 1 40831 479 1 eBook

978 1 40830 987 2 pb
978 1 40831 478 4 eBook